TEAM SPIRIT

BY ROBERT R. O'BRIEN
ILLUSTRATED BY RICK BROWN

Harcourt

Orlando   Boston   Dallas   Chicago   San Diego

Visit *The Learning Site!*

www.harcourtschool.com

Today is Jay's first day at our school.
He just moved here from South Korea. He
doesn't speak much to anyone, even our
teacher, Mr. Hanna.

2

During our social studies lesson, Mr. Hanna asked Jay about South Korea. Jay smiled and said, "I do not know many English words." Still, Jay pointed to South Korea on the map of the world.

Later, Mr. Hanna asked Jay to solve a
math problem. Jay smiled a little. He said,
"I do not know many English words." Still,
Jay went to the board and did the
problem.

At snack time, Ben, Cassie, and Lee sat
next to Jay. They tried to talk to him about
his new life. "I do not know many English
words," he said. Still, Jay offered to share
his snack.

At recess, we picked teams for a game
of kickball. Jay waited to get picked. He
didn't smile at all. Everyone was sure he
would not know how to play!

Our team was in the field first. Lisa, the captain, asked Jay if he could play in right field. Jay said, "I do not know many English words." Still, he walked out to right field and waited.

At first, our team was playing badly. We couldn't stop the other team. Their kickers kept getting base hits.

All of a sudden, there were runners on two bases. One was at first base. The other was at second. A kicker kicked the ball hard.

The ball went right by the pitcher. It flew
into right field. Jay ran to the ball, picked
it up, and threw it to second base. One
runner was out!

Sally Schultz was their next kicker. She was the best player in our whole class! Everyone on their team was shouting. Everyone on our team was quiet.

Sally kicked the ball high into the air. It looked like a home run. Jay ran back and back and back. He turned around and caught the ball!

Quickly, Jay threw the ball to second
base. The runner at second base was out!
Jay had gotten a double play!

Everybody on our team was cheering for Jay. He smiled when he came in from right field. Now, it was time for our team to kick.

Our kickers did well. We were catching up. The bases were loaded. There were two outs. It was Jay's turn to kick.

Jay kicked the ball over the fence. It was a home run! We had won! We all cheered. Jay cheered, too. He had a big smile on his face. Guess what? He didn't have to say a word!